A Runaway Tale

PRAISE FOR *STORYSHARES*

"One of the brightest innovators and game-changers in the education industry."
– Forbes

"Your success in applying research-validated practices to promote literacy serves as a valuable model for other organizations seeking to create evidence-based literacy programs."
- Library of Congress

"We need powerful social and educational innovation, and Storyshares is breaking new ground. The organization addresses critical problems facing our students and teachers. I am excited about the strategies it brings to the collective work of making sure every student has an equal chance in life."
– Teach For America

"Around the world, this is one of the up-and-coming trailblazers changing the landscape of literacy and education."
- International Literacy Association

"It's the perfect idea. There's really nothing like this. I mean wow, this will be a wonderful experience for young people."   - Andrea Davis Pinkney, Executive Director, Scholastic

"Reading for meaning opens opportunities for a lifetime of learning. Providing emerging readers with engaging texts that are designed to offer both challenges and support for each individual will improve their lives for years to come. Storyshares is a wonderful start."
- David Rose, Co-founder of CAST & UDL

A Runaway Tale

Jaclyn Westlake

STORYSHARES

Story Share, Inc.
New York. Boston. Philadelphia.

Copyright © 2022 by Jaclyn Westlake

All rights reserved.

Published in the United States by Story Share, Inc.

The characters and events in this book are fictitious. Any similarity to real persons, living or dead, is entirely coincidental.

Storyshares
Story Share, Inc.
24 N. Bryn Mawr Avenue #340
Bryn Mawr, PA 19010-3304
www.storyshares.org

Inspiring reading with a new kind of book.

Interest Level: High School
Grade Level Equivalent: 3.9

9781642614619

Book design by Storyshares

Printed in the United States of America

Storyshares Presents

1

He knew they'd be looking for him. But Zigg was an expert at evasion. And, on the chance that he was caught, he could fight. Father had seen to that.

It was a cold, gray day. The sun hid behind a thick wall of clouds, and the breeze carried a tinge of winter. It blew through the tall thicket of trees where Zigg hid. He shivered. He was used to living outside, preferred it even. But he was not accustomed to going without food. And Zigg was starving. It had been at least three days since his last meal, and his stomach groaned in protest. Hiding out in the woods wasn't going to be a long-term solution. Fighter or not, Zigg wasn't much of a hunter. And he needed to eat something soon.

He'd do anything for some chicken. Or bacon.

Mmm. Bacon.

Zigg pushed his anxiety about being spotted aside and emerged from the safety of the forest.

Going into town was risky, but he didn't have a choice. Curling up and dying just wasn't in his nature. And he certainly couldn't go back home. Not that he wanted to.

A small, two-lane highway led the way to town. Gravel crunched under Zigg's feet as he carefully navigated the shoulder, being sure to stay close to the woods that sandwiched the road. It wasn't a long walk, but he took his time. It was best to avoid drawing attention to himself.

He walked several miles until a sleepy trailer park, the first sign of civilization, gave way to neatly kept suburbs. It was early. He didn't see anyone except a lone paperboy whizzing by on his bike. He'd been here before, when he was very young. That was a long time ago. Most of his life had been spent on Father's land. And in the basement. Zigg hated thinking about the basement.

A sprinkler kicked on, catching Zigg in its crossfire.

He probably needed a bath, but not like this. It was that kind of neighborhood. The type of place with freshly cut grass, automatic sprinkler systems, paper boys, and locked doors. The gentle pieces of his soul, the ones that remained, quietly longed to walk through the door of one of these houses and into the loving, open arms of a family. And maybe some bacon. Part of Zigg still longed for a home.

He needed to get downtown. That's where the food would be. He stuffed weak thoughts of family and warmth and delicious treats down and pushed himself forward. He didn't have much farther to go.

Brick buildings and flickering streetlights dotted the simple downtown avenues. There were more people here, opening shops for the morning, emptying trash bins, and exchanging friendly hellos. Zigg stood on a corner, taking it all in. A part of him longed to run up to these strangers and ask for help. But he didn't know who he could trust. It was best to stay out of sight.

The smell of freshly baked bread and grilled breakfast meats tortured his stomach. No more hesitating. He needed to find food.

He made his way to a small alley behind a row of restaurants and carefully picked his way down the narrow, dumpster-lined path. He knew he'd find someone's leftovers here. And he certainly wasn't above scrounging through garbage for a meal. Sure enough, he found a pile of burnt muffins that had fallen out of an overly stuffed trash bin. He ate them ravenously.

As Zigg was preparing to devour his fourth muffin, the back door to the bakery swung open. He froze. A tall, portly man in a stained white apron stared down at him. "Hey! Get out of there!" the man yelled.

Zigg didn't hesitate. He ran, hoping the man hadn't recognized him. If he had, it wouldn't be long before Father showed up.

2

A full belly and a fading rush of adrenaline are enough to exhaust anyone. And Zigg was no exception. He didn't know how long he'd been asleep, but he woke with a start. His makeshift hideout in the downtown park bushes wasn't nearly as secure as the forest. Zigg was suddenly acutely aware of that. He needed to move.

He crept out from under the bush and stretched his legs. Stifling a yawn, he began walking toward the suburbs. If he could make it back to his wooded hideout, he could regroup and make a longerterm plan. Sneaking into town every couple of days wasn't going to work. He'd be no freer than when he was with Father.

That's when he heard it.

A large, black van screeched to a halt behind him. Zigg looked over his shoulder in time to see two men in dark clothing jump out of the vehicle. They were holding weapons.

He'd been found.

Zigg ran. He was quite the sprinter and could easily outpace just about anyone. Especially Father. As he ran, Zigg flashed back to the escape. The moment he became a runaway.

At first, Father had kept him in chains, like the others. But with time, Zigg had gained his father's confidence and was trusted to spend more time outside on his own. Being Father's most prized fighter had its privileges. But Zigg was terrified. He'd seen others brutally punished for a lot less than running away. And he wasn't sure he could risk it.

He planned his escape gradually. First by testing the boundaries of where he could roam. He'd disappear into the woods surrounding Father's compound for just a few minutes at a time. Proof that he could be trusted to come home. He began to truly know the forest. He knew all the best hiding spots. He knew the places where the soft forest floor and thick brush would allow him to move silently, invisibly. There in the woods, Zigg allowed himself to dream of freedom.

He may never have gone through with his plan had it not been for that day. He'd been slinking through the woods when Father emerged from the basement. He was dragging one of Zigg's brothers. Zigg watched silently, helplessly, as Father beat his brother until he no longer moved. Zigg was sure he was dead. And he knew that someday, if he stayed, he would be too.

So, he ran. Just like he was running now.

Zigg slowed his pace as he reached the outskirts of town. Panting, he looked over his shoulder and saw no one. He breathed a sigh of relief.

"Gotcha."

Zigg felt a thick, coarse rope slide around his body. A rough hand slammed over his mouth. A surge of sheer terror washed over him. It was the men from the van.

He thrashed violently as a restraint tightened around his neck. Zigg was fierce, but the men were too strong. They were pros. And he was outnumbered. But he kept fighting, yelling as he was forced into the back of their unmarked van. Even after the door slammed shut.

Then everything went black.

3

Zigg woke to find himself in a stark, square cell. His head pounded from whatever drugs the men had used to sedate him. But that was nothing compared to the pit in his stomach. Just like that, he'd lost his freedom. Again.

From the bars of his cage, Zigg tried to look around. He was in some sort of facility, lined with identical concrete cells. Each cell housed a prisoner like him. He didn't recognize anyone.

He needed to get out of there. Zigg began carefully tracing the walls of his small cell, looking for cracks, holes, or weak spots. He clawed at the corners and dug at the floor.

It was solid cement.

Panic began to set in. Zigg was trapped. And he wanted answers. He yelled at the top of his lungs. He pounded against the bars of the cell. Men in dark clothes, his captors, passed by, acting as if they didn't hear him at all. They talked amongst themselves in a language he couldn't understand.

Zigg's head spun with endless questions. Why was he here? What did they want with him? Did Father know he was here?

He didn't know how much time had passed. Eventually, a man with a serious face and a stocky build appeared in front of Zigg's cell. He slid a tray of food under the bars, turned on his heel, and walked away. Zigg threw the tray across the room.

Maybe it was the terror, hunger, or exhaustion, or some combination of it all, but Zigg was done being tough. At least for tonight. He stopped pacing the length of his tiny cell and collapsed onto the thin, scratchy mat in the corner. Heaving a deep sigh, he finally let the weight of it all go. And he began to cry.

4

He never did find out why he was there.

The days became routine. So much so that they were difficult to keep track of. Mornings began with a brief walk outside (with his restraints tightly fastened, of course) and a trip to the bathroom. Then, a dry, flavorless breakfast back in his cell. Sometimes his captors would forget about him, and Zigg would be forced to go in the corner of his cage.

He passed most of the time staring out through the bars of his cell. Watching his captors come and go, bringing new prisoners in and old ones out. He never knew where they went. Some would come back, but others he never saw again. Either way, no one ever talked to him about it.

The nights were the worst. The facility was cold, damp, and eerily silent, save for the stray whimper of another lonely inmate. After his evening walk, bathroom break, and dinner scraps, Zigg would lay on his mat, willing sleep to take him away.

But first, he usually thought about the past.

Before Father, before the ring, before the forest and his capture, Zigg had been happy. He'd once been surrounded by brothers and sisters, and a mother who loved them. A family.

He'd played in the yard, carefree. He'd wrestled with his siblings and napped in the warm sun. He was different then. But that was before. That was all so long ago.

Zigg would never forget the night Father broke into his home and lured him from his bed. If only he'd known what Father wanted with him, what he would do when he got Zigg into the basement. Zigg would have fought like hell.

But Zigg had gone willingly. A gullible youngster.

Could he ever be happy again? Not here, that was for sure. This place was gray and cold.

Loud, harsh, and hopeless. Why was he even here? Did they know how many he'd killed?

Perhaps this was his punishment.

He certainly deserved it.

A Runaway Tale

5

Zigg was restless. He itched to fight. He would snap at the other inmates as they passed his cell, trying to scare them. He could tell who had been in a ring, like him. Only a few. They were the ones who triggered him most. Self-restraint wasn't his strong suit. Once in a while, a scrappy prisoner would give him a reaction. And even though Zigg couldn't get to him, the rush of it all made him feel alive.

Fighting, for Zigg, was complicated. When Father first took him in, he'd hated it. He was terrified. But refusing to fight didn't spare him pain. Either his opponent would issue a punishing beat down or worse, Father would later.

With time and practice, Zigg became great. He was a natural; the perfect combination of strength, stealth, and wits. He was light on his feet and could easily anticipate his opponent's next move. Like he was psychic, Father had said. He zigged when his sparring partner zagged. That's how he got his name.

Zigg won every fight Father entered him in. He crushed every opponent. He even killed a few, he was sure. But he never saw any of them again.

The spectators, though, he came to know quite well. They were regulars, all of them. Mostly loud, drunk, raucous men who got their jollies watching youngsters fight. And Zigg was their favorite. They cheered him on wildly and celebrated his wins. They basked in the defeat of Zigg's opponents. In those moments, Zigg loved them.

But later, back in his room, as he recovered from his injuries or thought about whoever he'd hurt that night, Zigg hated himself. He felt like a monster. And he was trapped.

It was possible, Zigg thought, to love something and to loathe it all at once. That was fighting. It would always be a part of him.

A Runaway Tale

6

He looked tough. He knew that. Despite his youth, Zigg was all muscle. Short but stout, with a scarred face that he'd once been told was handsome, dark features and soulful brown eyes. His build, his tough exterior had served him well when he'd fought for Father in the basement. When he'd become champion of the ring.

Here, in this new place, one sudden move could make most of his captors jump. And Zigg liked it that way. It was a small piece of freedom; a distant feeling of control over his world. At least he could scare them.

But Zigg had also developed an uneasy trust with a man called Jim. At least as much as one can trust a person who holds them against their will. Jim had a kind face and a calm demeanor. He didn't manhandle Zigg like some of the other captors had. He gave Zigg space. Against his better judgment, Zigg liked Jim. And he thought Jim might like him, too.

Jim called Zigg "Tiger" and he had no idea why. But he didn't really care. He could be Tiger.

Leaving Zigg behind didn't sound like such a bad idea, anyway. His life here was rigid and cold. But at least they left him alone.

Father hadn't shown up yet. So maybe he was safe here. And there was food. Even if it was bland.

Jim became Zigg's primary handler. He would bring Zigg breakfast, lunch, and dinner every day. Sometimes, he'd even sneak Zigg scraps of bacon or bread. With time, Zigg stopped protesting when Jim attached the restraints. They'd take a quiet walk to the bathroom or around the yard of the facility. They never really spoke. Jim wouldn't understand what Zigg was saying anyway.

7

Once, Zigg slipped out of his restraints and bolted, running faster than he'd ever run before. But the fence surrounding the perimeter of his prison was too tall, and he couldn't make it over. He was quickly caught.

But Jim didn't punish him.

Occasionally, Zigg had to endure a mortifying bath or medical examination. Worse, he'd sometimes be led into a room filled with waiting strangers who would poke and prod him. He never learned why. But Jim was always there, guiding Zigg through whatever plans the day held for him – mundane, humiliating, or otherwise.

"I know, I know," Jim would say as he led Zigg back

to his cell.

"This isn't easy."

He lost track of the days. It had probably been several months since he was captured, robbed of his freedom. But he couldn't be sure.

Jim's visits weren't always predictable. Today he showed up early. After lunch but before dinner.

"Let's go, Tiger."

Jim attached Zigg's restraints. Together, they walked calmly down the noisy hall. Zigg knew the drill. Strangers would be waiting behind a big metal door, ready to examine him.

Before the door swung open, he felt a familiar pit in his stomach, afraid that his father had finally tracked him down. He'd be brutally punished for running away and then promptly entered in a fight. As soon as his wounds had sufficiently healed, of course.

8

A man and a woman were waiting on the other side of the door. They looked young, clean, and untouched by hardship. They might as well have been from another planet. Zigg retreated to his usual corner and stared them down, gritting his teeth.

"This is Tiger," Jim said as he settled into a chair. "He's not much of a social butterfly."

The woman smiled and knelt to look Zigg in the eye. "Hi, Tiger," she purred gently. She seemed kind. But that didn't mean anything to Zigg. He looked away.

He hung back in the corner, watching the man and the woman talk with his captor. Zigg didn't speak their language, but he'd picked up a few words during his captivity. And he knew they were talking about him.

"He doesn't get along well with the others," Jim said.

"He's been through a lot," the man replied. The woman nodded in agreement.

"He doesn't seem very interested in either of you," Jim observed.

"It'll take time," said the woman.

"Well, he's all yours then, if you'll have him," Jim replied with a shrug.

The woman turned and addressed Zigg directly. "Do you want to come with us?" she asked, as if he had a choice. Zigg just stared.

"It's your lucky day," Jim said.

9

Zigg, still in restraints, was led out of the facility by the man and woman who walked lightly, happily toward the parking lot. The fresh air and new scenery should have been thrilling.

But Zigg was broken. He'd been in the facility for so long, wondering what the purpose of it all was, that he just couldn't bring himself to care. He'd come to peace with the fact that his life simply wasn't his own. His fate was in the hands of others. Whatever destiny he was heading toward next, he was sure it was nothing to get excited about.

But he might miss Jim a little, he thought.

The man opened the door to a small, gray car. He

gestured for Zigg to get into the back seat. Zigg did so, begrudgingly. He allowed the woman to fasten a soft, loose restraint around his chest. Then, she gently touched his head. Zigg leaned into it, ever so slightly, surprised by how good a kind hand felt. It had been a long time since he'd felt anything like it. Sometimes he wondered if he ever really had.

After she finished fastening his restraints, the woman dug around in her bag and pulled out a piece of bacon. She handed it to Zigg, who promptly gobbled it down. It would take more than bacon to win him over, but it was a start. He wondered if Jim had told these people how much he loved the stuff.

The woman closed the door and climbed into the front seat. The man started the car. And just like that, they drove away. Away from the prison. Away from Jim. Away from the ghost of Father.

It had been months since he'd been in a car. How much time had passed since his capture? He couldn't be sure. The woman rolled the windows down. Zigg felt a surge of excitement as the fresh air whooshed all around him. He breathed in the infinite scents of the outside world. He felt himself relax, just a little.

They drove for a while. The man and the woman talked amongst themselves, but the woman would turn and check on Zigg every once in a while, smiling her kind smile. Zigg settled into the soft seat. He didn't know why, but he felt relieved.

The open window called to him. Testing the pull of his restraints, Zigg crept toward it.

Climbing up on the door's armrest, he gingerly stuck his head out the window. A rush of cool air washed across his face. His ears flew back with the force of the wind. He felt alive, free even. And for the first time in a long time, his tail wagged.

The woman looked back and smiled. She placed her hand over the man's and said, "I think we should call him Lucky."

Zigg liked that.

A Runaway Tale

About The Author

Jaclyn Westlake is a human resources manager turned career advice columnist turned aspiring fiction writer, which is what she really wanted to do all along.

When she's not crafting fanciful tales, you can probably find her browsing a bookstore or paddle boarding with her adorable dachshund, Indiana Jones. She lives on a boat in the San Francisco Bay Area with her husband Brian.

30

About The Publisher

Story Shares is a nonprofit focused on supporting the millions of teens and adults who struggle with reading by creating a new shelf in the library specifically for them. The ever-growing collection features content that is compelling and culturally relevant for teens and adults, yet still readable at a range of lower reading levels.

Story Shares generates content by engaging deeply with writers, bringing together a community to create this new kind of book. With more intriguing and approachable stories to choose from, the teens and adults who have fallen behind are improving their skills and beginning to discover the joy of reading. For more information, visit storyshares.org.

Easy to Read. Hard to Put Down.

Made in the USA
Monee, IL
27 January 2023